To: LIAM _____TT

My GOOD
GRANDSONS

LOVE,

GRANDMA
+
GRANDPA
CHUCK

The Good in Me From A to Z by Dottie

by Lisa Blecker

Co-illustrated with C. Aaron Kreader

Library of Congress Control Number: 2009925702

ISBN#978-1-931492-26-3

Hardcover Edition

Board Book Edition first printed in 2006

13 12 11 10 09   6 5 4 3 2 1

Discover Writing Press
www.discoverwriting.com

Shoreham, VT

Book design by C. Aaron Kreader

Printed in China through Asia Pacific Offset

The Good in Me From A to Z
by Dottie

by
Lisa Blecker
Co-Illustrated with C. Aaron Kreader

Dedicated to my mom, Marianne Blecker.

Special thanks to Jay Braden, Susan Engle, Lawrence Kreader, Amanda P. Sevak, the Spirit of Children Conference, and Linda Popov for her groundbreaking work in character education.

Active when I jump about

Beautiful inside and out

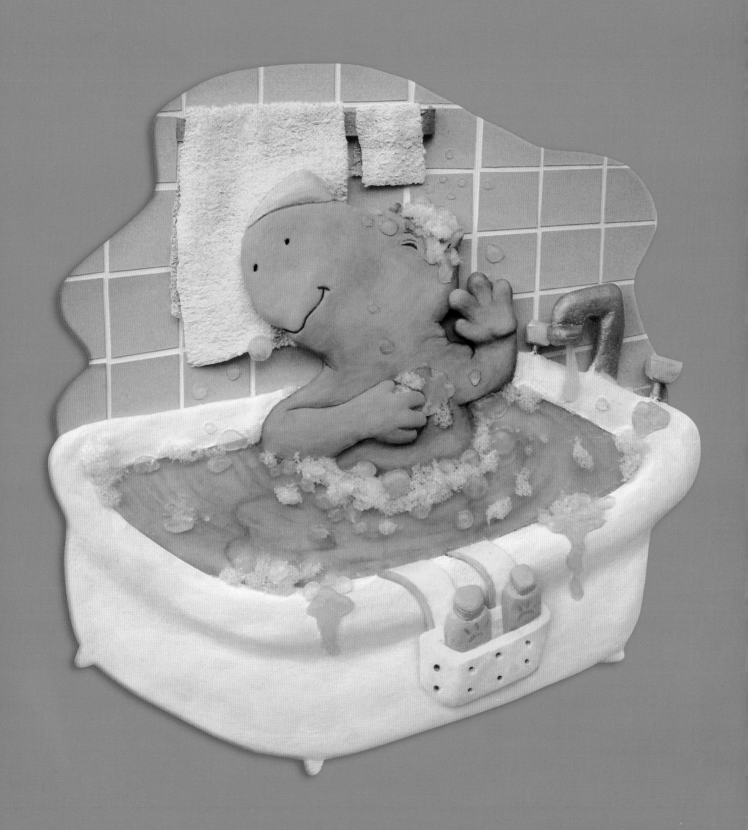

Courageous when
I face a fear

Determined to
succeed this year

Encouraging my friend to try

Friendly when I'm saying hi

Generous when I give a gift

Helpful when I stir and sift

Independent when
I go to school

Joyful when I'm in the pool

Kind when I like to share

Loving when I show I care

Moderate when
I watch one show

Nurturing so my flowers grow

Orderly with my supplies

Patient when my brother tries

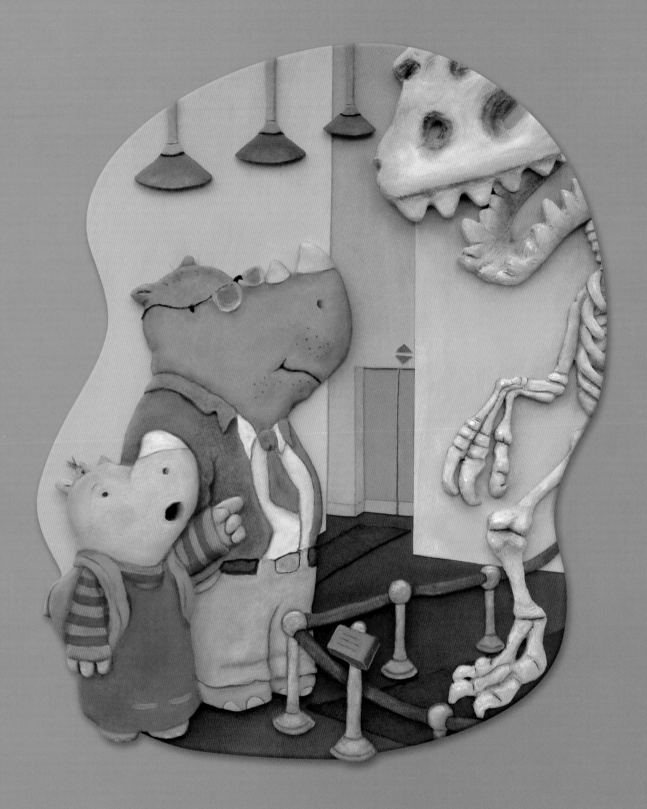

Questioning so I understand

Respectful when I raise my hand

Supportive when a friend is hurt

Truthful when I track in dirt

Uniting when I make a friend

Victorious when
I reach the end

Wise with all I Know

eXcellent at sculpting dough

Yielding when I look both ways

Zany in my silly plays

Now I've gone the whole way through,

The Good in Me by

Your name: _____

won't you share the good in you!